American Indians

TALL BOY AND THE COYOTE

By Edna Walker Chandler

Pictures by Jack Merryweather

Benefic Press • Chicago
ATLANTA, DALLAS, LONG BEACH, PORTLAND

Contents

Library of Congress
Number 61-7680

Tall Boy Can Help

This is Tall Boy.
The hogan is his home.

Blue Flower is
his mother.

She makes rugs.
Little Bird helps
make rugs.

Blue Flower and
Little Bird make
good rugs.

Running Bear is his father.
Running Bear works in the corn.
He takes water to the hogan.
Tall Boy likes to help his father.

Turtle Man
is big.
He is the
big brother.

Small Frog is little.
He helps with Baby Brother.

Here is Tall Boy with his dog.
Tall Boy likes to play with his dog.

Running Bear
said, "I will work
in the corn today."
"May I help with the corn?"
said Tall Boy.
"No," said his father,
"You will go with the sheep again.
That is your work."

"You will take
the sheep to find
grass and water,"
said Running Bear.
Tall Boy did not
want to go with
the sheep.

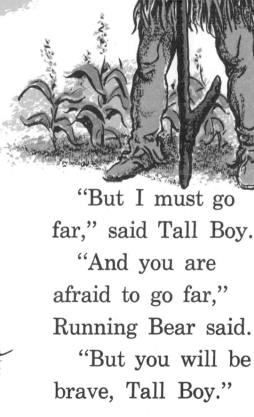

"But I must go
far," said Tall Boy.
"And you are
afraid to go far,"
Running Bear said.
"But you will be
brave, Tall Boy."

Tall Boy Takes the Sheep

Tall Boy said, "I am not brave.
But I will go with the sheep.
I want to be brave, Father."

Tall Boy did
not want to
go alone.

Tall Boy looked
at his dog.

"Come," he said.
"Come with me.
You will help me.
You will play
with me, too."

Little Bird said,
"Tall Boy will want
to eat.
Here is something
good to eat."
"Thank you," said
Tall Boy.
"When the sun is
far up I will want
something to eat."

"Look out for Coyote,"
said Running Bear.
"Coyote is bad for the sheep.
Do not be afraid of him.
Make him go away."

Little Bird said,
"May I go with Tall Boy, Mother?
I like to help with the sheep."
"I want you to help me,"
said Blue Flower.
"We will make a rug."

Tall Boy went
with the sheep.
His dog went
with him.
But they did not
go far away.

Tall Boy Is Afraid

The sun went down.
Tall Boy went home with the sheep.
Running Bear said,
"Did you see Coyote today?"
"No," said Tall Boy.
"Good!" said Running Bear.

Little Bird helped Blue Flower.
Small Frog helped with Baby Brother.
Then Blue Flower said,
"Come, Small Frog.
You and Baby Brother come.
He wants to eat.
We all want to eat."

Running Bear said,
"Now we will go to sleep.
Day will come soon.
Then you will go with the sheep
again, Tall Boy."
Tall Boy went to sleep.
His dog went to sleep, too.

Something came near the hogan.
"Oh, I hear something!
I am afraid," said Tall Boy.
"Father! I hear something.
It may be Coyote!" he called.

Running Bear looked.
"I see Owl," he said.
"Owl is good."
Tall Boy said,
"I did not know it was Owl.
I am not afraid of Owl."

Day was here.

It was time to work and time to play.

"Come, Tall Boy," said Running Bear.

"You must get the sheep.

You must take them to good water.

You must go far."

24

Tall Boy went
to get the sheep.
Something ran
out of the pen.

Tall Boy ran
to the hogan.
He ran fast.

"Something was
in the pen!" said
Tall Boy.
"It came out
of the pen.
I do not know
what it was."
"And you are afraid,"
Running Bear said.
"Look!
That is what
you saw."

Running Bear said to Blue Flower,
"I want Tall Boy to herd the sheep.
But he is afraid all the time.
He can not be a good herder.
What will we do?"
Blue Flower said, "A time will
come for Tall Boy to be brave.
He will not be afraid then.
You will see."

Tall Boy and the Sheep

"Mother, may Little Bird go
with me?" asked Tall Boy.
"She can help with the sheep."
"No," said Blue Flower.
"Little Bird will help me."

"You must go
alone!" Running
Bear said.

"Turtle Man and
I must work
in the corn.

When the sun is
down, I will come.

Turtle Man and
I will find you."

Tall Boy and his
dog went with the
herd of sheep.
They went alone.
They went far,
far away.

They looked and
looked for good
grass and water.

Then they saw some grass.

"Here is some grass,"
said Tall Boy.

"The sheep can eat this grass.
Water is here too."
Then he looked at his dog.

"But what will we do?"
said Tall Boy.

The dog saw something.
He ran and ran.
"Good!" said Tall Boy, "Run fast!
I want to sleep.
But Coyote may
come here.
I must not
sleep then.
What can I do?"

"I know!" said Tall Boy.
"I will play that I am brave.
I am not afraid at all.
See!
I am not afraid of Coyote!"

Tall Boy said,
"I will do this!
I am not
afraid of them."

"The coyotes all
went away," said
Tall Boy.

"I am brave.
I made all the
coyotes go away."

"They all went
away, away, away,"
he said.

Where Are My Sheep?

Tall Boy heard something!
Now he did not sleep.
"I hear my dog!" he said.
"The dog is afraid.
Where is he?
Where are my sheep?"

Tall Boy looked
and looked.

"I am not a good
herder," he said.

"Where are my
sheep now?"

He ran and ran.

He looked here.

He looked here.
No sheep!
No dog!

Then Tall Boy heard something.
It was his dog.
"I hear you," he said.
"I will come to you.
I will come fast."

Tall Boy
ran fast.
   He ran up, up.
   "I see the sheep!"
said Tall Boy.
   "Something is with them.
Coyote is down there!"

"Go away!" said Tall Boy.
"Go away.
You are bad!"
The coyote did not run away.
He did not go away at all!

Then Tall Boy
did something.
"You will go
away!" he said.
"I will make
you go away!"
Tall Boy did
it again and
again and again.

"You want the little sheep,"
said Tall Boy.
"You can not have it."
Coyote went away.
But he did not go far.

Tall Boy ran to get a big rock.
"Now you will go away!"
said Tall Boy.
The rock did not go far.
It was too big.

"What can I do?" said Tall Boy.
"What can I do now?
I can run to Coyote.
But he is not afraid of me.
I am afraid of him.
Coyote knows I am afraid.
What can I do?"

What Did Tall Boy Do?

Then Tall Boy saw something.
"What a big, big rock!" he said.
"Now I can do something.
I know what I can do!"

"This is work," he said.
"But I can do it."
Tall Boy worked and worked.
The coyote wanted the sheep.

At last
Tall Boy
did it.
The rock
went down,
         down,
               down.

Coyote ran fast.
"See Coyote go!"
said Tall Boy.
"He can run fast."
"Now I will get my sheep,"
said Tall Boy.
"My sheep are afraid.
My dog may be afraid, too.
But I am not afraid."

Tall Boy went down.
He went to the big rock.
He saw something.
"Oh, oh!" said Tall Boy.
"Coyote did not take this."

"See this!" Tall
Boy said to his dog.
"My father will
see this, too.
He will know
that I saw Coyote.
He will know I
was not afraid."

"Come!" Tall Boy said to his dog.
"Help me with the sheep.
They are afraid.
We must get all the sheep."

Tall Boy worked
and worked.
His dog worked
and worked.
"The sheep are
all here now," said
Tall Boy.

Tall Boy Is Brave

The sun went down.
Running Bear came to Tall Boy.
Turtle Man came with him,
"Here you are," said Running Bear.
"The sheep are here, too.
You did good work, Tall Boy."
Turtle Man said, "Did Coyote come?"

"Yes, Coyote came," said Tall Boy.
"Look! Coyote did not want this.
Now I have it.
Come! You will see.
You will see where Coyote was."

Tall Boy went to the big rock.
Running Bear looked and looked.
Turtle Man looked, too.
They heard what Tall Boy said.
They saw what the rock
did to Coyote.

Running Bear said,
"You are not afraid.
I can see that.
You will not be afraid again.
You are brave now.
You will be a good herder."

"I was afraid of Coyote,"
said Tall Boy.

"Then I looked at the sheep.
They were all afraid.
I wanted to help them.
I did help them.
I was not afraid then."

"It is not bad
to be afraid," said
Running Bear.
"But it is bad
to run away.
You did not run
away from Coyote.
You made him run.
And you have this!
Coyote will not
come to get the
sheep again."

"We will go now," said Running Bear.
"Blue Flower and Little Bird will
want to see what you have.
They will want to know
that Tall Boy is brave."

Vocabulary

The total number of different words used in this book is 113. Of these, 95 are below first-grade level. The nine words shown below in roman type are first-grade words, and those in italics are above first-grade. The numbers indicate the pages on which the words first appear.

afraid   11

alone   11

bad   17

brave   11

brothers   17

corn   7

coyotes   36

for   17

grass   11

hear   22

heard   37

herd   27

herder   27

hogan   5

pen   25

rugs   6

rock   45

sheep   10

today   10

More About Indians

The early Navajo Indians were largely rov-
ing tribes, depending upon hunting for their
livelihood. Occasional raids on farming settle-
ments supplemented their supplies when game
was scarce.

Sometime during the eighteenth century, the
Navajos grew more sedentary as they gradu-
ally gave up hunting for sheep-herding. They
were nomadic in the respect that they moved
about with their stock, searching for suitable
grazing lands. They followed established
routes, however, maintaining summer and win-
ter homes near their seasonal pastures. Fami-
lies planted gardens and orchards at the summer hogans. Hogans were built of earth, logs,
and rocks.

Navajos learned the art of weaving from the
Pueblo Indian groups, and after the introduc-
tion of sheep by the Spaniards, blanket-making
became an important part of Navajo life.

The first Navajo weaving was done with yarn unraveled from Spanish woolen cloth. Later, between 1850 and 1870, cheaper, dyed yarn was imported, and Navajo weaving showed an increase in output and popularity. It was also during this period that rugs became the principal product of their looms.

Navajos became silversmiths around the middle of the nineteenth century, after a Mexican craftsman introduced them to his art. Silver work is done by the men, while weaving is left to the women.

Today, the Navajos comprise the largest Indian nation in the United States. Their huge reservation spans sections of Arizona and New Mexico. Their lives present an interesting combination of contemporary civilization and traditional tribal customs.

Navajo rugs and silver products enjoy worldwide fame.